SALISBURY
FREE
LIBRARY

BY Mary Jessie Parker

ILLUSTRATED BY Shannon McNeill

Dutton Children's Books

NEW YORK

LIBRARY OF CONGRESS CATALOGING-IN-PUBLICATION DATA

Parker, Mary Jessie.
Wild and Woolly / by Mary Jessie Parker; illustrations by Shannon McNeill.—1st ed.
p. cm.
Summary: Wild, a bighorn sheep, and Woolly, a ranch sheep, decide to try each other's lives, but find that they prefer their own, after all.
ISBN 0-525-47276-2
[1. Sheep—Fiction. 2. Friendship—Fiction.
3. Self-acceptance—Fiction.] I. McNeill, Shannon, date. II. Title.
PZ7.P22735Wi 2005 [E]—dc22 2003019236

Published in the United States by Dutton Children's Books,
a division of Penguin Young Readers Group
345 Hudson Street, New York, New York 10014
www.penguin.com

Designed by Tim Hall • Manufactured in China
First Edition
1 3 5 7 9 10 8 6 4 2

For Kevin, who is a
little bit wild and very woolly
—M.J.P.
For David
XOXO —S.M.

The high, rocky hill baked under the hot sun. Wild, a bighorn sheep who lived on the high, rocky hill, baked too—from hoof to head.

The grassy field below baked under the hot sun. Woolly, a ranch sheep who lived on the grassy field, baked too—from head to hoof.

Wild noticed the shade of the woods below him.

Trot,

trot,

trot.

Down to the shady woods he walked.

Woolly noticed the shade of the woods above him.

Plod . . .

plod . . .

plod . . .

Up to the shady woods he climbed.

Wild saw Woolly on the path in the shady woods.

"Snort!" said Wild. "You are a curious animal. I've never met anyone like you."

"Blaaat!" said Woolly. "I am Woolly. I am a sheep."

"A sheep?" snorted Wild. He looked at Woolly, hoof to head. "You don't look like the sheep I know. Where is your brown coat? Where are your curly horns?" Wild shook his curly horns. *Whoosh-whoosh.*

"I don't know," said Woolly, "but I am a sheep. I live on the grassy field." Woolly pointed down to his grassy field.

"Hmmm," said Wild. "This is curious."

"*You* are curious," said Woolly. "I've never met anyone like you, either. What are you?"

"I am Wild," said Wild. "I am a sheep."

"A sheep?" asked Woolly. "You don't look like the sheep I know. Where are your fat legs? Where is your curly wool?" Woolly shook his woolly ears. *Flippity-flap.*

"I don't know," said Wild, "but I am a sheep. I live on the high, rocky hill." Wild pointed up to the high, rocky hill.

"Hmmm," said Woolly. "This is curious."

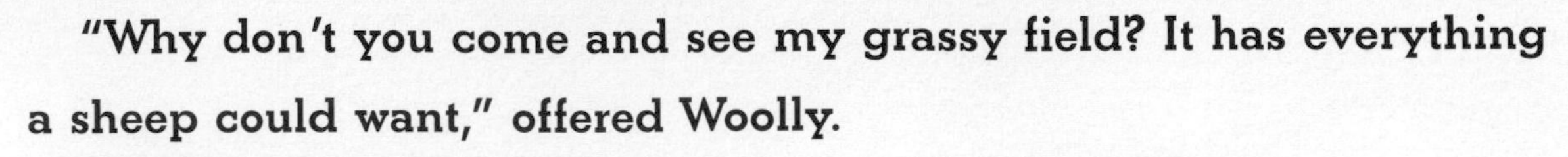

"Why don't you come and see my grassy field? It has everything a sheep could want," offered Woolly.

"I will," said Wild.

Woolly led Wild down to the grassy field.

Plod . . . plod . . . plod . . .

Trot, trot, trot.

"This is it," said Woolly, rolling and wriggling in the grass.

Wild looked around. "There are no bulging boulders to hide behind."

"No," said Woolly. "Just grass."

"You are too woolly to hide in the grass," said Wild.

"But," asked Woolly, "why would I hide?"

"Because of hungry wolves and . . ." Wild's eyes popped open wide!

A low, dark shape ran toward them across the grassy field. Wild pointed behind Woolly. "Behind you! Run, Woolly, run!" shouted Wild.

Wild ran fast. Trot, trot, trot.

Woolly tried to run fast. Plod . . . plod . . . plod . . .

"What is behind me?" shouted Woolly.

"A wolf!" answered Wild.

"A wolf? Behind me? Oh my! *Blaaat!*" Woolly tried to move his legs faster.

"He is right beside you!" shouted Wild. Wild pointed beside Woolly.

Woolly looked . . .

and stopped. So did the low, dark animal.

"Stop, Wild," panted Woolly. "This isn't a wolf. This is a *dog*."

"A dog?" Wild snorted and stamped his hooves. "What is a dog?"

"I am a dog. *Ar-r-r-f!"* said the dog.

Wild saw many sharp teeth twinkling inside the dog's *arf*. Wild shook his curly horns. *Whoosh-whoosh.*

"Wait!" said Woolly. He stepped between them. "Stop!"

They stopped. "A dog keeps us sheep safe from the wolf," said Woolly. "This dog is my friend, Picket. Picket, this is Wild. He is visiting the grassy field. Wild thought you were a wolf."

"A wolf? *Hardy-arf-arf,*" laughed Picket. "How could you mistake me for a wolf? A wolf has sharp teeth and a long tail. A wolf! *Hardy-arf-arf.*"

Wild looked at Picket's sharp teeth and long tail. "My mistake," said Wild as he rolled his eyes.

Picket sniffed Wild. "I've never smelled anyone like you."

Wild rolled his eyes again. "I am a sheep," he snorted. *Whoosh-whoosh.*

"You don't look like the sheep I know," said Picket. "Are you a distant cousin?"

"Not too distant," said Woolly. "He lives on that high, rocky hill." Wild and Woolly pointed to the high, rocky hill.

"Nice to meet you, big fella," said Picket. Picket turned to Woolly. "So long, little buddy." He gave Woolly a long, wet lick.

"*Baa-ha-ha!* That tickles!" Woolly shook his woolly ears. *Flippity-flap.*

"So long, Wild." Picket gave Wild a slick lick too. "*Hardy-arf-arf.*" Then across the field he ran. Race, race, race.

Wild wiped his face with his hoof.
"The grassy field is not the place for me."

"But smell the haystacks," said Woolly, "and see the pretty green grass that goes on and on. The grassy field has everything a sheep could want."

"Not *this* sheep," said Wild. "I should head home."

"Oh," said Woolly.

"Come with me," offered Wild. "Come visit my home on the high, rocky hill. It *really* has everything a sheep could want."

"I will," said Woolly. His eyes looked across the flat, grassy field and up, up, up to the high, rocky hill. He sighed.

Wild led Woolly through the shady woods. Up the high, rocky hill Wild tramped. Up the high, rocky hill Woolly trudged.

Trot, trot, trot. Plod . . . plod . . . plod . . .

They walked through fragrant balsams. Woolly sneezed. They climbed steep cliffs. Woolly wheezed.

"Are we there yet?" panted Woolly.

"No," said Wild. "Not yet."

They hurdled fallen logs. Woolly huffed. They hiked around bulging boulders. Woolly puffed.

"Are we there yet?" panted Woolly.

"No, not yet."

They ducked under low branches. Woolly dipped. They sloshed through muddy puddles. Woolly slipped.

Trot, trot, trot. Plod . . . plod . . . plod . . .

Finally Wild said, "We are there."

"*Blaaat!* This is a very high and very rocky home." Woolly looked at his hooves. "And very earthy too." Woolly lifted each hoof and shook off mud and leaves and needles. "Where is your water tank?"

"Follow me," said Wild. Wild led the way through clumpy bushes to a small pool near the edge of the cliff.

Woolly tried to follow Wild.

He pushed and pulled and pulled and pushed, but his curly wool was caught in the clumpy bushes.

"I am stuck!" shouted Woolly. He began to cry. "I will never see my grassy home again!"

"You can see it right now," said Wild. He pointed over the cliff's edge to the grassy field below. "It's right there."

Woolly looked down, down, down to his grassy field.

He bawled.

Wild sighed. "I will help."

Wild gnawed sticks here. Wild gnawed sticks there. He snipped above Woolly, and he snipped below Woolly. He trimmed by Woolly's left side. He trimmed by Woolly's right side.

With a big grunt, Woolly wriggled free. He looked into the small pond. "My curly wool!" cried Woolly. "I look like a porcupine! The high, rocky hill is *not* the place for me."

"But smell the balsams," said Wild, "and see the mountaintops that go on and on. The high, rocky hill has everything a sheep could want."

"Not *this* sheep," said Woolly. "I should go home."

"Oh," said Wild.

Wild helped Woolly down the high, rocky hill to the shady woods below. They stopped on the path. Woolly looked at Wild. Wild looked at Woolly.

Wild smiled. "Sooo, Woolly, how was your day?" he teased.

"How was yours?" Woolly teased back. He smiled at Wild.

The two smiles changed into two grins.

The two grins turned into two big laughs.

"Baa-ha-ha! Baa-ha-ha!" they laughed.

They laughed and laughed and laughed until their eyes filled with laughing-tears.

Wild wiped his eyes. "Tomorrow?"

Woolly wiped his eyes. "In the woods."

Whoosh-whoosh. Flippity-flap.

That night, the air was cool and sweet.
Wild settled by his bulging boulder.
Woolly settled by his haystack.
They both fell asleep . . .

. . . counting sheep.